STUART LITTLE™

Think Big, Vote Little!

Adaptation by Laura Driscoll

based on the teleplay "Life, Liberty, and the Pursuit of

Taco Tuesday" by Kevin Hopps

Illustrations by Thomas Perkins

📚 HarperFestival®

A Division of HarperCollins*Publishers*

It was not fair.

It was not right.

In the school cafeteria, Taco Tuesday was now *Fish Stick* Tuesday!

Yuck!

Stuart, George, and Will had to

do something!

Stuart had an idea.

Larry Gronk was running for
class officer.

"Maybe Larry can bring back
Taco Tuesday!" said Stuart.

Stuart asked Larry about it.

But he didn't care.

"And Taco Tuesday isn't the only

problem around here," George said.

The lockers often jammed.

The playground was a mess.
They needed a class officer
who would fix those things.
Somebody like . . .

"You, Stuart!" said Will.

Before he knew it, Stuart was
running for class officer, too.

The whole Little family helped out.
They made posters, buttons, and
cookies to help Stuart get votes.

Stuart handed out cookies at school.

"Think big: vote Little!" he said.

But Larry Gronk gave away

cake and ice cream!

How could Stuart top that?

George came up with a new

plan for Stuart.

"We need action!" said George.

The students would forget the cookies and the buttons. Instead, Stuart would solve the school's *real* problems!

George had the idea

for Stuart to start a petition.

If lots of kids signed it,

they could bring back

Taco Tuesday!

George's next idea

was to fix the lockers.

When a locker jammed,

Stuart came to the rescue!

Then George had the idea

to clean up the playground.

They worked all afternoon.

The schoolyard was spotless!

George had tons of great ideas.

"Why didn't *you* run for class officer, George?" Stuart asked.

George shrugged.

"Who'd vote for me?" he said.

The next morning, Stuart, George, and Will wanted to show off the playground.

But—oh, no!

Someone had messed it up!

It was even messier than before.

"I know who did this!" Will said,

as they cleaned up *again*.

"Gronk!"

He thought Larry did it to make Stuart look bad.

If so, it seemed to be working.

But only for a few minutes.

Then the principal announced

Taco Tuesday was back!

Stuart's petition had worked!

"Yes! We did it!" said Will.

A group of kids picked Stuart up.

"Stu-art! Stu-art!" they chanted.

Now Stuart seemed sure to win.

The school was about to vote.

Stuart and Larry had one last

chance to speak to the school.

Larry spoke first,

and surprised everyone.

"I don't think you should

vote for me," he said.

Larry admitted that he was the one
who messed up the playground.
"I'm really sorry," he said.

Stuart surprised everyone, too.
"I don't think you should vote
for me, either," he said.
"We should all vote for my brother,
George!"

Stuart explained that George had thought of all the great ideas: the petition, the lockers, and the playground cleanup.

Everyone cheered for George.

"George! George!" they chanted.

Stuart smiled.

George was happy.

Stuart was proud.

And their motto still worked:

Think big: vote Little!